TIME TRAILS

RAINFOREST

BY LIZ GOGERLY AND ROB HUNT
ILLUSTRATED BY ØIVIND HOVLAND

W

FRANKLIN WATTS
LONDON • SYDNEY

TIMELINE

All dates are approximate.

4.6 BILLION YEARS AGO TO 541 MILLION YEARS AGO

EARTH FORMS!
ARCHEAN
PROTEROZOIC

PALAEOZOIC 541–251 MILLION YEARS AGO

CAMBRIAN
ORDOVICIAN (EARLY, MIDDLE, LATE)
SILURIAN (LLANDOVERY, WENLOCK, LUDLOW, PRIDOLI)
DEVONIAN (EARLY, MIDDLE, LATE)
CARBONIFEROUS (PENNSYLVANIAN, MISSISSIPPIAN)
PERMIAN (CISURALIAN, GUADALUPIAN, LOPINGIAN)

MESOZOIC 251–65.5 MILLION YEARS AGO

TRIASSIC (EARLY, MIDDLE, LATE)
JURASSIC (EARLY, MIDDLE, LATE)
CRETACEOUS (EARLY, LATE)

CENOZOIC 65.5 MILLION YEARS AGO TO PRESENT DAY

PALEOGENE (PALAEOCENE, EOCENE, OLIGOCENE)
NEOGENE (MIOCENE, PLIOCENE)
QUATERNARY (PLEISTOCENE, HOLOCENE)

CONTENTS

WHAT AND WHERE ARE RAINFORESTS?

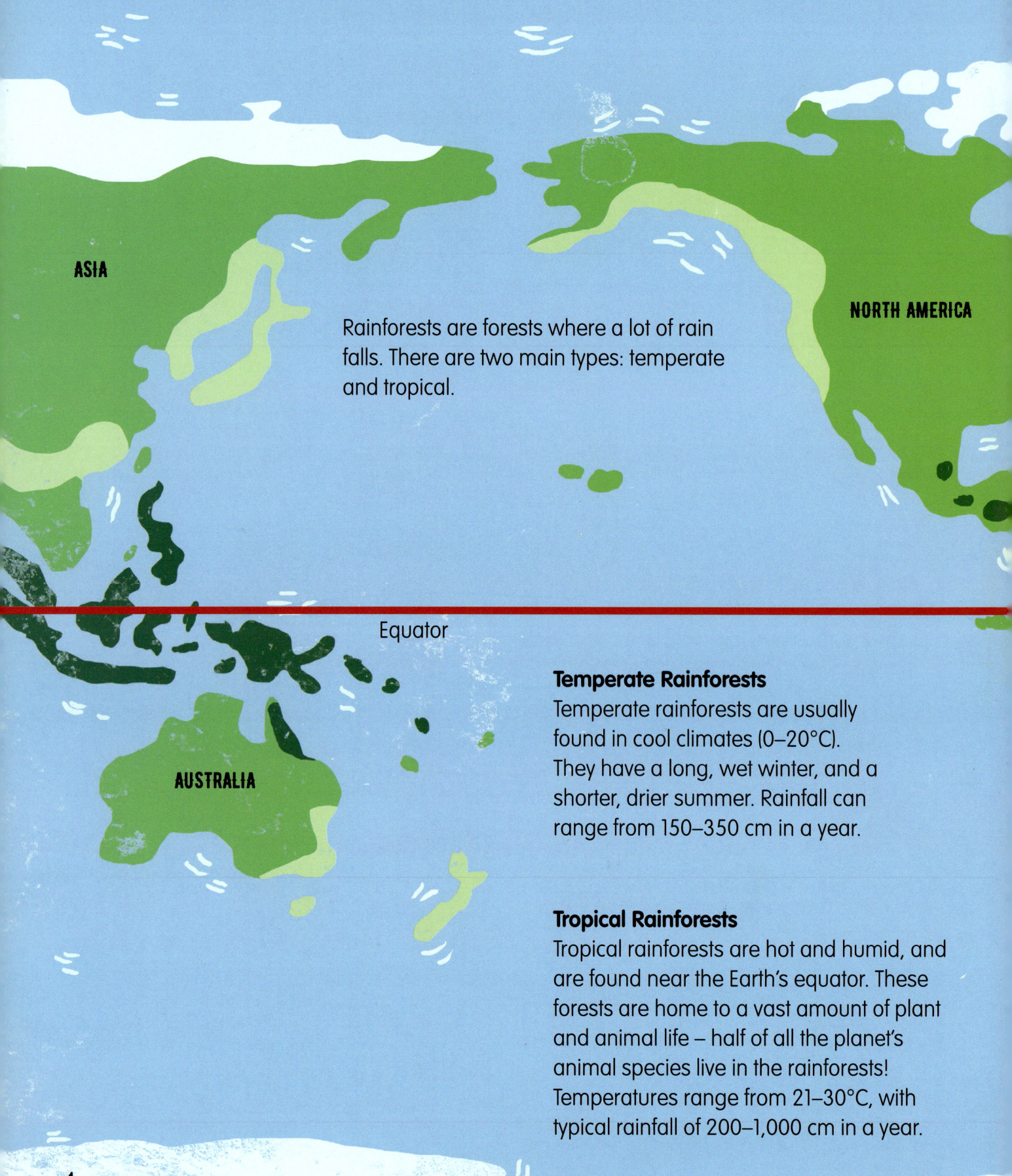

ASIA

NORTH AMERICA

Rainforests are forests where a lot of rain falls. There are two main types: temperate and tropical.

Equator

AUSTRALIA

Temperate Rainforests
Temperate rainforests are usually found in cool climates (0–20°C). They have a long, wet winter, and a shorter, drier summer. Rainfall can range from 150–350 cm in a year.

Tropical Rainforests
Tropical rainforests are hot and humid, and are found near the Earth's equator. These forests are home to a vast amount of plant and animal life – half of all the planet's animal species live in the rainforests! Temperatures range from 21–30°C, with typical rainfall of 200–1,000 cm in a year.

EUROPE

AFRICA

Amazon
rainforest

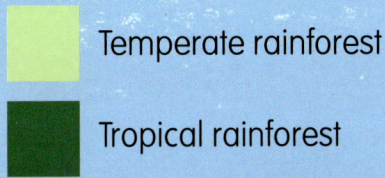

SOUTH AMERICA

The Amazing Amazon
The Amazon is the world's
biggest tropical rainforest. It
is estimated to have around
40,000 different types, or
species, of plant, 1,300 bird
species, 3,000 fish species,
430 mammal species, and
2.5 million insect species. It
is also home to between 400
and 500 Amerindian tribes,
some of which have never
had any contact with the
outside world.

This is the story of how the
rainforests have developed
over millions of years to be one
of the most vital features of
planet Earth. Let's explore ...

DEVONIAN
417-354 MILLION YEARS AGO

Developments in the Devonian
During the Devonian period plants began to spread from swamps and seas onto the land. Over millions of years, the landscape changed as forests grew, becoming home to many animals.

Plant and all life forms originally developed in the water in the form of algae.

The Devonian period is sometimes called the age of fish as the seas are full of many types of sea creature.

The sky is filled with insects, as several species have evolved to be able to fly.

The first plants to inhabit the land do not have roots. These early plants are mosses and liverworts (and are still around today). They cling to rocks using root-like hairs and they reproduce using spores.

Over the centuries, more complex plants called ferns evolve. These plants have roots and vessels to absorb and transport water and nutrients. This enables them to grow much taller.

At the start of the Devonian period, ferns grew to about 30 cm tall. By the end of the period they were forming forests over 30 m high! These Wattieza have the first woody trunks, but have fronds rather than leaves, and like all the other plants at this time, they reproduce by releasing spores.

These 6–8-m tall Prototaxites may look like tree trunks, but they are actually enormous fungi.

During the Carboniferous period that followed, many forests collapsed and died due to volcanic eruptions and climate change. They formed a layer in the earth, which turned into coal.

PERMIAN
290–248 MILLION YEARS AGO

The Land of the Conifers

After the dramatic collapse of the first rainforests during the mass extinction that occurred in the Carboniferous period, a new type of plant evolved called the conifer.

Conifers, along with ginkgos and cycads, are among the first spermatophytes, meaning they produce seeds.

Ginkgos grow upwards to about 10 m before spreading out their branches. They need lots of water and are often found by streams.

Cycads, like conifers and ginkgos, are early gymnosperms. Gymnosperm means 'naked seeds', because these plants' seeds do not have any covering, unlike modern nuts and berries.

PEAT

COAL

The wind blows pollen from one plant to another, fertilising the seeds. Insects, such as scorpion flies and beetles, may well have helped with the pollination.

Conifers, with their needle-like leaves and ability to survive for a long time without water, thrive as the climate warms and cools.

At the end of the Permian period more animals and plants are wiped out than at any other time in Earth's history. Nobody knows what causes the Great Dying – perhaps volcanic eruptions or global warming. One thing is for sure, it will take the forest millions of years to recover.

JURASSIC
205–142 MILLION YEARS AGO

Scattering the Seeds

During the drier Triassic period (248–205 million years ago) seed-producing plants took a while to recover from the Great Dying. By the Jurassic period these plants began to grown again. Dinosaurs and some small mammals also started roaming the Earth.

The forests are still mainly conifers. Each species evolved ways to spread their seeds – a process called seed dispersal. By the Jurassic period, plants have found many different ways to do it …

This dinosaur has been eating cycad seeds. It eventually needs a poo. The seeds drop at a new site, complete with fertiliser!

Ginkgos often grow by streams. Their seeds drop into the water and flow away from the parent plant to grow elsewhere.

Araucariaceae and Pinaceae trees produce winged seeds from their cones, which catch the wind and blow away.

Some plants just use the weight and shape of the seed to help with dispersal. Larger seeds could simply drop and roll away.

Some seeds are sticky or have burrs. They get stuck to animals and eventually drop off far from the parent plant.

There are still many plants, like these horsetails, that reproduce with spores instead of seeds. The spores are mainly dispersed by the wind.

CRETACEOUS
142–66 MILLION YEARS AGO

Flower Power

At the end of the Cretaceous period, parts of the Earth were ablaze! Known as the Chicxulub Impact, a 10-km-wide asteroid struck an area which is now in Mexico. Rainforests surrounding the site caught fire.

Many plants were wiped out by the fire, tsunami, earthquakes and climate change that occurred after the asteroid impact. When the plants eventually recovered, the flowering plants that had evolved earlier in the Cretaceous period took advantage of the new growing conditions and flourished.

Some trees, like these pine trees, develop a new type of seed dispersal. They store their seeds for a long time until there is a trigger, such as fire, which releases them. They begin to grow when the fire has passed.

Many modern trees, including figs, planes and magnolias, appear during the Cretaceous period, but manage to survive the mass extinction event.

One group of dinosaurs does manage to survive – to become the ancestors of birds. It's possible that their larger brains and toothless beaks may have helped them to find food after the impact event.

Early forms of grass have been found in the fossilised dung of grazing dinosaurs, like this Titanosaur. However, none of these dinosaurs will survive for long after the Chicxulub Impact.

Archaefructus is one of the earliest flowering plants (angiosperms). Angiosperms are plants that have seeds inside fruit.

This early type of pitcher plant, called Archaemphoria, may be carnivorous. Pitcher plants trap insects in their cupped leaves, where they die and decay. The plant absorbs the decayed material.

The ancestors of modern mammals survived by staying underground as the temperatures above rose.

13

EOCENE
55–33.7 MILLION YEARS AGO

Global Warming

At the beginning of the Eocene period, there was global warming, allowing rainforests to grow everywhere, even at the North and South Poles. Several million years later, the climate cooled and became drier. Rainforests shrank to areas around the equator. As the continental plates moved, the supercontinent called Pangaea separated into the continents we recognise today.

This sandy rain has blown across the Atlantic Ocean from the Sahara region of Africa. The Sahara dust contains phosphorus, which helps plants to grow well.

In what is now South America, the Andes mountains form. This reverses the flow of the River Amazon, so that it now empties into the Atlantic Ocean. This is probably what led to the growth of the Amazon rainforest.

Deciduous trees are better than coniferous trees at coping with seasonal temperature changes, and begin to overtake the evergreen tropical species.

Newly-evolved grasses only grow near to river banks and lake shores.

Butterflies feed on flowering plants.

Midway through the Eocene period, monkeys appear in South America – but nobody knows how they got there from Africa. They possibly island-hopped across the Atlantic Ocean by floating on plants that had been swept out to sea.

MIOCENE
23.8–5.3 MILLION YEARS AGO

A Struggle for Survival
Conditions were cooler and drier in the Miocene period and rainforests struggled to survive. They no longer covered as much of Earth. This led to more diversity amongst animals in different parts of the world and an increase in dry forests and woodlands.

Sebecosuchia is an ancestor of the modern crocodile. These deadly animals have serrated teeth and a powerful jaw.

Thylacosmilus is a type of sabre-toothed marsupial.

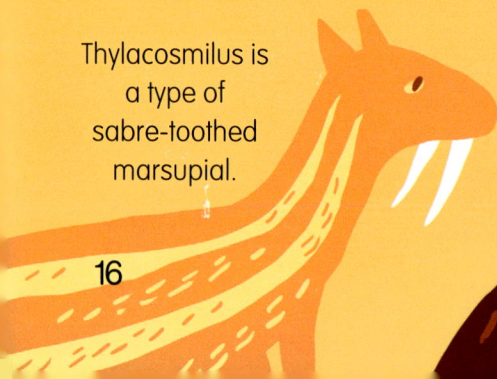

Paraphysornis (terror birds) are fierce creatures. They measure around 2 m in length but have tiny wings so they can't fly.

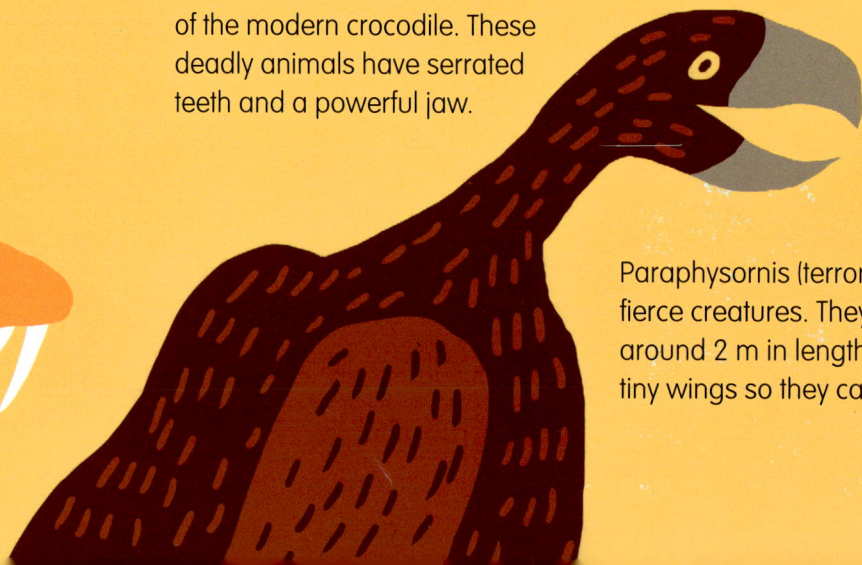

The monkeys are adapting to life in the Amazon unaware that thousands of kilometres away in Africa some of their relatives are becoming more like humans – something that will hugely affect the very distant future.

Lurking in the River Amazon is the giant caiman, one of the largest species of crocodile of all time.

Phoberomys is a giant rodent.

· PARAPHYSORNIS ·

Macranhinga are giant fish-eating birds. Also known as snakebirds, these creatures probably use their sharp beaks to dart their underwater prey.

PLEISTOCENE
2.6 MILLION TO 11.7 THOUSAND YEARS AGO

A Cooling-off Period

The planet was in the grip of an ice age, but it was still tropical at the equator where rainforests survived. The monkeys that lived in South America were quite small. Across the Atlantic, their relatives were much bigger and one group of primates, called humans, were starting their journey out of Africa.

This giant ground sloth is called Megalonyx. The name means 'giant claw'.

Smilodon, often called a sabre-toothed cat, lies in wait to pounce on plant-eating animals like Megalonyx.

There are four levels to the rainforest. The **emergent layer** is the highest, and contains the tops of the tallest trees.

The **rainforest canopy** contains most of the plant and animal life. It blocks most of the sunlight from the lower levels.

The third layer is called the **understory**. It is home to lots of birds, snakes and lizards, as well as the creatures that like to eat them such as jaguars.

The bottom layer is called the **forest floor** and contains the decomposers. Organisms, such as fungi and insects, break down dead things, such as fallen leaves.

HOLOCENE
11.7 THOUSAND YEARS AGO TO PRESENT

The Arrival of the Humans

Over the last few thousand years, nomadic tribes of humans have been moving from their original home in Africa. Eventually, about 11,000 years ago, some made it to the Amazon – an epic trip! Their arrival changes everything.

The new arrivals catch and cook animals and eat them with the wide variety of fruit and vegetables found in the forest.

The monkeys are hunted by their close relatives – the humans!

The rivers are full of piranhas. Tribesmen collect the razor-sharp teeth from these fish and use them to make tools and weapons.

Crocodiles, snakes, jaguars and humans all like to eat capybaras, the world's largest rodents.

The poison dart frog makes poison in glands in its skin. Amazon tribespeople wipe the darts for their blowpipes in the poison before going hunting.

· POISON DART FROG ·

21

HOLOCENE
11.7 THOUSAND YEARS AGO TO PRESENT

The Changing Jungle
Almost as soon as humans arrived they began to make changes.

Rainforests grow well because they recycle dead material. However, the soil is low in nutrients, making it bad for farming. To make it more fertile, humans add charred wood to the soil. This allows the tribes to grow crops in forest clearings.

Rainforest tribes discover what they can and can't eat. Some, such as the spiked pepper, prove to be medicinal. The leaves are used to stop bleeding.

The Chachapoya tribe live in the cloud forests of the Amazon between 900–1450. They are fearsome fighters but they are conquered by the mighty Incas.

The Incas build cities and towns and farm crops such as potatoes, quinoa and corn to feed their growing population.

The Incas make sturdy boats out of reeds. They use them to navigate lakes and rivers.

In this village they are farming cassava, also known as manioc, a very important source of energy.

THE EUROPEAN INVASION
1492–21ST CENTURY

An Unwelcome Visitor

The arrival of European explorers at the end of the 15th century is a disaster for the Amazon tribespeople. The Spanish, with their superior weapons, quickly conquer the Inca Empire and begin mining and harvesting the region for its resources.

Many people are enslaved, and many die from the poor treatment they receive or the diseases they pick up from the Europeans.

Enslaved people are forced to do tough work, such as mining.

Machu Picchu was built as a citadel for an Inca emperor. It was abandoned by the Incas soon after the Spanish arrived, possibly because most of the inhabitants caught smallpox from the invaders and died.

Francisco de Orellana is the first European to navigate the length of the River Amazon. His crew are often attacked by local tribespeople.

When fighting one tribe, he is so surprised to see female fighters that he calls them Amazons, after the female warriors from Greek mythology. This may have given the River Amazon its name.

Rumours spread about a city of gold called El Dorado. Explorers search all over South and Central America for it. They never find it, but they discover lots of other places.

Brazilwood is very highly prized around the world. It is useful for making a type of red dye. The wood proves to be so important that the country Brazil is named after it.

The Spanish are shocked to discover that the Incas sacrifice children to their gods. This convinces them to force the Incas to become Roman Catholics.

ANTHROPOCENE
PRESENT DAY

Close to Disaster

For thousands of years Amazon tribespeople farmed in the rainforest and ate what they needed before moving on. This allowed the forest to recover and grow again.

The balance all changed once Europeans arrived. They began to take too much from the forest and parts of the rainforest were lost forever.

Slash-and-burn farming is a method where areas of the rainforest are cut down and burned to enrich the soil.

Slash-and-burn works on a small scale, but now it's being done on a huge scale. It can lead to deforestation, soil erosion and extinctions.

Brazil is building hydroelectric dams to generate clean, renewable energy. Renewable energy is a good thing but rainforest ecosystems can be damaged during their construction. Huge areas are flooded as the dams start to work.

Cutting down trees is illegal in protected areas of the rainforest. However, illegal loggers continue to destroy parts of the rainforest just to get the valuable trees they can sell.

Red-faced monkeys called bald uakaris are one of the many endangered species in the Amazon rainforest.

STOP SLASH AND BURN!

SAVE TREES!

NO MINING!

Rainforests are vital for the survival of many species of plant and animal, but are under constant threat from human-made problems such as mining, logging and climate change.

INTO THE FUTURE

Save the Rainforests

In recent years, people have become more aware that we must save the Amazon rainforest. If we destroy the rainforests then the whole world suffers. In Brazil there are more protected areas than ever and laws against rainforest crime are enforced.

Although it is threatened, the rainforest is so vast and uncharted that new species are always being discovered. The thimble frog and the spaghetti passion flower have been discovered recently.

Many important medicines have been developed from trees and plants growing in the rainforests. Other medicines could be developed from plants not yet discovered.

Seeds have been collected to be kept in a seed store in the Arctic Circle. If there is a major catastrophe, like the asteroid strike that wiped the dinosaurs out, these seeds will give us a chance of restoring plant life.

Activists, scientists and many governments are working together to save the rainforests. One of the ways is through ethical and sustainable farming of products like chocolate. You can check labels to make sure what you are consuming is ethically produced.

The rate of deforestation is still alarming but it is slowing down. At last, governments are beginning to understand how vital the rainforest and its resources are to our planet.

GLOSSARY

Ancestor: A plant, animal or living organism that is related to or descended from similar in the past.

Asteroid: A rocky body which orbits the Sun and is smaller than a planet but larger than a meteoroid.

Blowpipe: A weapon in the shape of a tube with which arrows or darts are shot by blowing through it.

Canopy: Usually well over 30 m above the ground, this leafy layer is like the roof of the rainforest.

Carnivorous: Describes an animal that feeds on meat.

Citadel: A castle or fortress often found on higher ground above or near a city.

Climate: The usual weather conditions that exist in an area in general or over a long period.

Cloud forest: A very wet forest that is usually high above sea level and is nearly always covered in cloud.

Conifer: A kind of tree or shrub that has cones with seeds.

Continental plates: The large pieces of the surface of the Earth that move separately. The Earth currently has seven large land masses, each known as a continent.

Cultivate: To prepare and use land for growing crops.

Cycad: A small group of plants, with large divided leaves, that was abundant in ancient times. They look like palm trees or tree ferns.

Deciduous: Used to describe a kind of tree or shrub that has leaves that fall off at the end of the growing season.

Disperse: To spread or scatter something over a wider area.

Diversity: When something has a great deal of variety.

Emergent: Describes the highest level where the tops of trees poke out from the rainforest canopy below.

Equator: An imaginary east-to-west line around the middle of the Earth. It divides the Earth into the Northern Hemisphere and the Southern Hemisphere.

Evolve: To change from one form to another over time and over many generations.

Extinction: The state of certain species when they have died out and stopped reproducing entirely.

Fertilise: To reproduce a plant or animal by introducing the male pollen or sperm to a female seed or egg.

Fertiliser: A natural substance (like dung or bone meal) or a chemical substance that is spread on land to help make plants grow well.

Forest floor: The lowest layer of the rainforest.

Fossil: The remains of a prehistoric animal or plant that has been turned to stone and preserved for millions of years.

Frond: The leaf or leaf-like part of a palm, fern or similar plant.

Ginkgos: Large trees with fan-shaped leaves that were abundant during the Jurassic period.

Global warming: The rising temperature of planet Earth is called global warming.

Great Dying: The period when 96% of species died out.

Gymnosperm: The most common kind of land plants during the Cretaceous and Jurassic periods. These seed-bearing plants (cycad, ginkgo, yew and conifers) had a cone with seeds rather than flowers or fruits.

Ice Age: A period of extended low temperatures on the Earth when the polar ice sheets expand and glaciers formed.

Jurassic: The period of Earth's history from 205 million–142 million years ago.

Lichen: A fungi that grows like a crust on trees or on the ground and can sometimes appear like tiny bushes.

Mammal: An animal that gives birth to live young and feeds them on its own milk.

Marsupial: A group of mammals whose babies are carried in a pouch on the mother's stomach.

Medicinal: Something such as a plant that has healing properties.

Navigate: To plan and travel across a stretch of land, ocean or along a river.

Nomadic: Describes a life spent wandering from place to place.

Nutrients: Vitamins and minerals that provide nourishment for living organisms.

Organism: Any individual living thing, such as an animal, plant or single-celled life form.

Phosphorus: A chemical element that helps plants grow well.

Pollination/pollinate: Pollen is a fine powder produced by the male parts of plants. It is often carried by insects or the wind to the female part of the same kind of plant to produce seeds (to pollinate) which is a process called pollination.

Primates: The group of highly intelligent and developed mammals that includes humans, monkeys and apes.

Renewable energy: Energy that is generated from renewable sources such as the sun or wind.

Reproduce: When plants or animals produce new life.

Sacrifice: The act of killing an animal or person to thank a god or deity for something.

Serrated: Having a jagged edge.

Species: A group of plants or animals that have the same appearance and can breed with one another.

Spores: Reproductive cells produced by certain non-seed bearing plants like ferns or fungi. Spores are asexual which means they do not need male and female cells to reproduce.

Temperate: Describes a kind of climate that has mostly mild temperatures.

Tropical: Relating to the tropics with a climate that is mostly hot and humid.

Understory: A lower layer of the rainforest. Above the forest floor and below the canopy this part of the forest gets little light so many of the plants have big leaves to survive.

FURTHER INFORMATION

Further Reading

Visual Explorers: Rainforests by Paul Calver and Toby Reynolds (Franklin Watts)

Look and Wonder: Incredible Rainforests by Kay Barnham and Maddie Frost (Wayland)

Explore!: Rainforests by Jen Green (Wayland)

Unstable Earth: What Happens if the Rainforests Disappear? by Mary Colson (Wayland)

The Where on Earth? Book of: Rainforests by Susie Brooks (Wayland)

Websites
www.natgeokids.com/uk/discover/geography/physical-geography/15-cool-things-about-rainforests/

Head to the National Geographic website for kids to find out some amazing tropical trivia and fascinating facts about the rainforest.

www.rainforest-alliance.org/kids

The message at the Rainforest Alliance is that you don't have to be big to make a big impact. This organisation encourages children to get involved saving the future of the rainforest. Check out the 10 easy ways that children can do their bit to help. There are plenty of plant and animal facts here too!

www.oddizzi.com/teachers/explore-the-world/physical-features/ecosystems/rainforests/rainforest-climate/

Clear and informative, this website is a must for children wanting to discover more about the layers of the rainforest, the plants, the people, the fascinating food and medicine and just about anything else that goes on in the rainforest. Photographs and gripping video footage bring the rainforest to life.

www.youtube.com/watch?v=JEsV5rqbVNQ

There are lots of videos of the rainforest on YouTube; this virtual field trip means you can explore the rainforest without leaving your classroom or home. Facts are backed up with diagrams, maps, fantastic photographs and jungle sounds!

INDEX

Franklin Watts
First published in Great Britain in 2019 by
The Watts Publishing Group
Copyright © The Watts Publishing Group 2019
All rights reserved

Illustrator: Øivind Hovland
Design manager: Peter Scoulding
Executive editor: Adrian Cole
ISBN 978 1 4451 5851 8
Printed in China

MIX
Paper from
responsible sources
FSC
www.fsc.org
FSC® C104740

Franklin Watts
An imprint of Hachette Children's Group
Part of The Watts Publishing Group
Carmelite House
50 Victoria Embankment
London EC4Y 0DZ

An Hachette UK Company
www.hachette.co.uk
www.franklinwatts.co.uk